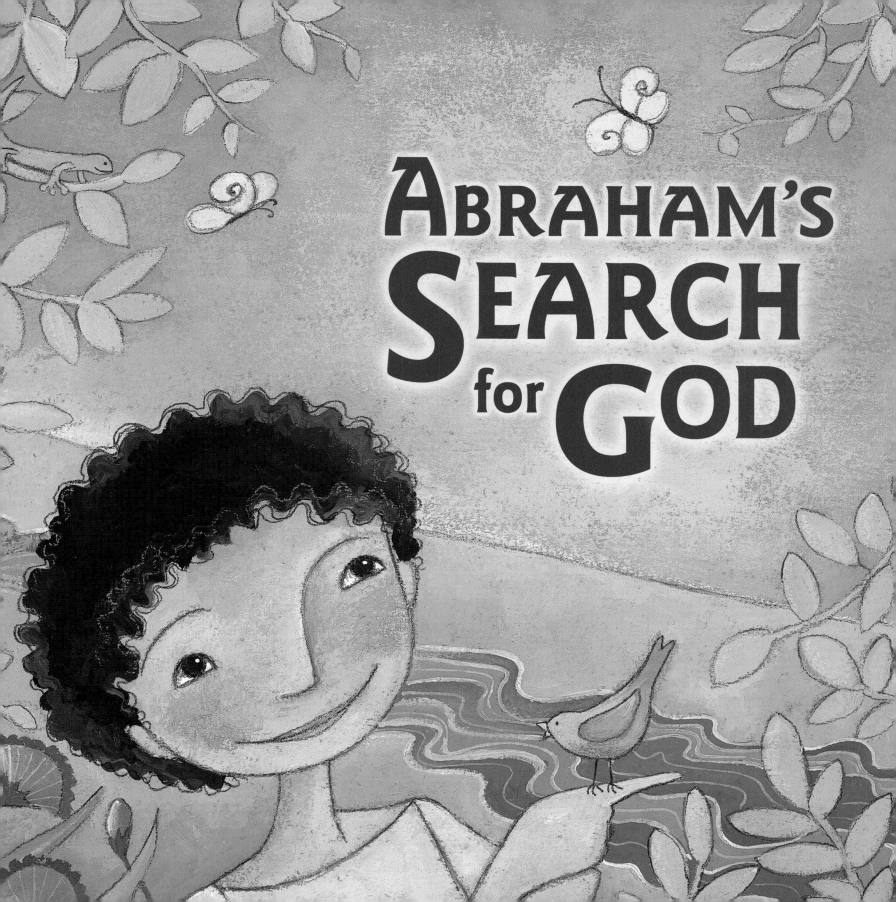

ABRAHAM'S SEARCH for GOD

To Kevin and Helene,
May your joy increase from year to year. —J.J.

To Greta and Leonardo with love. —N.U.

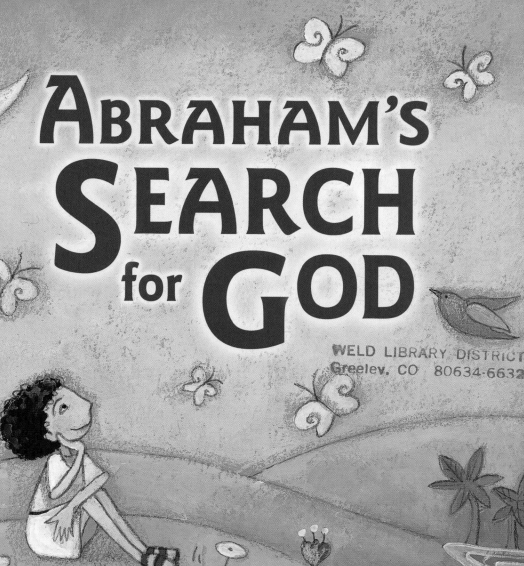

ABRAHAM'S SEARCH for GOD

by Jacqueline Jules   Illustrated by Natascia Ugliano

KAR-BEN
PUBLISHING

**Thousands and thousands
of years ago**, a boy named Abraham
lived in the city of Ur.

At that time, people prayed to idols, statues made out of clay and stone. People could not imagine believing in one God no one could see. Idols came in all different shapes and sizes. Some looked human, and some looked like animals. People brought idols into their homes and bowed down to them.

Even as a boy, Abraham was different. He felt silly when his father asked him to bow down and pray to stone statues.

"Idols have mouths but cannot speak to me. They have ears but cannot hear me. How can an idol help me?" Abraham asked.

His father scolded him. "Don't question our ways."

But Abraham continued to ask questions. Who made the clouds? Who made the flowers? The more Abraham questioned, the more he disliked the idea of praying to idols.

"There must be something greater than the idols," Abraham decided.

Abraham spent as much time as he could in the countryside. He loved climbing trees and listening to birds. He would lie in the grass for hours and watch the clouds float across the sky.

One summer day, Abraham stayed outdoors so long that night fell. The sudden darkness frightened him. Then a full moon came out, surrounded by millions of glittering stars.

Abraham raised his arms toward the moon. "I've found something greater than the idols—a shining silver light that lifts the darkness."

Abraham prayed to the moon:

Oh moon that lights the skies. You fill my heart and eyes.

He was so fascinated by the moon's beauty,
that he watched it all night.

But in the morning, the moon disappeared. The clouds turned pink, then red. Abraham watched a blazing ball of fire rise up in the eastern sky.

"I was wrong about the moon," Abraham said. "The sun lights up the entire earth and makes everything warm. It must be the ruler of everything and everyone."

Abraham bowed his head and prayed to the sun:

Oh sun that lights the skies. You fill my heart and eyes.

But then clouds came and covered the sky.

"No!" Abraham shouted, as he watched the clouds,
waiting for the sun to push them away. But the
clouds stayed where they were, blocking the sun.

"If the sun cannot push the clouds away," Abraham
said, "the sun is not the ruler of the world, either."

The sky became darker and darker. It began to rain. Lightning flashed and thunder boomed. Abraham hid in a cave with his hands over his ears.

"Thunder! Thunder!" Abraham cried. "You sent away the sun and made the earth shake. Are you the ruler of the world?"

Abraham trembled in the cave until the thunder finally stopped.

When he peeked outside, he saw a giant band of colors in the sky. Red, orange, yellow, green, blue, and purple reached as far as Abraham could see.

"Beautiful rainbow," he called out. "Did you stop the thunder?"

A few minutes later, the rainbow vanished and the sun shone, stronger than ever. Soon, Abraham felt hot and sticky. He looked up at the sun, but was forced to look away.

"Brilliant sun!" Abraham exclaimed. "You are so bright and so powerful. No one can look at your face."

Abraham wondered if the sun might be the ruler of everything after all.

The day passed. Afternoon came and then dusk. The sun
fell lower and lower in the sky. Abraham watched the sun
disappear. Darkness came.

As the moon and stars appeared, Abraham realized something.
"The sun and the moon are taking turns! Who makes that happen?"

Abraham could not sleep that night. Instead, he thought about the way the sun and the moon shared the sky. He thought about the terrible thunder and the beautiful rainbow. When a rosy dawn broke in the eastern sky, Abraham came to a new conclusion.

"There is something greater than the sun and the moon and the thunder. There is something even more beautiful than the rainbow. One great power makes the sun and the moon take turns. One great power makes the rainbow follow the thunder. This great power rules the entire universe and sets everything in motion. This great power is the one true God."

But Abraham was still troubled. "Where is the one God of heaven and earth? And if I can't see God, how will I know God is there?"

Abraham looked around him. He saw red flowers blooming in a field. He heard birds singing in the trees. He felt a warm breeze on his face. Suddenly Abraham knew.

"God is everywhere. God is in everything. God is something we know with our hearts."

Joyful tears fell from Abraham's eyes. Every part of his being joined in prayer:

One God of earth and skies. You fill my heart and eyes.

From that time on, Abraham worshipped One God. When he grew up, he told others about his belief. People listened.

Today, we remember Abraham as the father of three great religions: Judaism, Christianity, and Islam.

Abraham's story, as told in the *Book of Genesis*, begins when he is an adult and leaves his homeland at God's request to journey to the land of Canaan. He is originally called Abram, but God changes his name to Abraham during the course of his story. There is nothing in the text about his childhood. The many stories that are told are from the midrash, written to explain and expand on the Bible. They propose that although Abraham lived in a society of idol worshippers, he worshipped only one God, even as a youth.

My sources include *A Child's Introduction to Torah* by Shirley Newman, *The Classic Tales* by Ellen Frankel, *Hebrew Myths: The Book of Genesis* by Robert Graves and Raphael Patai, *Legends of Abraham the Patriarch* by S. Skulsky, *Legends of the Bible* by Louis Ginzberg, and *One-Minute Jewish Stories* adapted by Shari Lewis.

Text copyright © 2007 by Jacqueline Jules

KAR-BEN PUBLISHING
A division of Lerner Publishing Group, Inc.
241 First Avenue North
Minneapolis, MN 55401 U.S.A.
1-800-4KARBEN

Website address: www.karben.com

Library of Congress Cataloging-in-Publication Data

Jules, Jacqueline, 1956-
   Abraham's search for God / by Jacqueline Jules ; illustrated by Natascia Ugliano.
      p. cm.
   Includes bibliographical references.
   ISBN-13: 978-1-58013-243-5 (lib. bdg. : alk. paper)
   ISBN-10: 1-58013-243-X (lib. bdg. : alk. paper) 1. Abraham (Biblical patriarch)—
Childhood and youth—Legends. I. Ugliano, Natascia. II. Title.
   BS580.A3J85 2007

   222'.11092—dc22   2006027429

Manufactured in the United States of America
1 2 3 4 5 6 7 – DP – 11 10 09 08 07 06